eOR Rabbit

WOL

Piglet

MEET ALL THESE FRIENDS IN BUZZ BOOKS:

Thomas the Tank Engine
The Animals of Farthing Wood
Biker Mice from Mars
Fireman Sam
Joshua Jones
Rupert
Babar

First published in Great Britain in 1995 by Buzz Books
an imprint of Reed Children's Books
Michelin House, 81 Fulham Road, London SW3 6RB
and Auckland, Melbourne, Singapore and Toronto.

Copyright © 1995 Michael John Brown, Peter Janson-Smith,
Roger Hugh Vaughan Charles Morgan and Timothy Michael Robinson,
Trustees of the Pooh Properties.
Published under licence from The Walt Disney Company
Adapted from *Winnie-the-Pooh*, first published 1926 and
The House at Pooh Corner, first published 1928.
Text by A.A. Milne and drawings by E.H. Shepard
Copyright under the Berne Convention.
Adaptation of the line illustrations and colouring by Arkadia
copyright © 1995 Reed International Books Ltd.
All rights reserved
ISBN 1 855 91463 8
Printed in Italy

Winnie-the-Pooh and the North Pole

From the stories
by A.A. Milne

Christopher Robin was
sitting outside his door,
putting on his big boots.

As soon as he saw the
big boots, Pooh knew
that an adventure was
about to begin.

"We are all going on an Expedition," said Christopher Robin.

"Going on an *Expotition*?" said Pooh eagerly. "I don't think I've ever been on one of those. Where are we going on this Expotition?"

"Expedition, silly old Bear. It's got an 'x' in it. We're going to discover the North Pole."

"What *is* the North
Pole?" Pooh asked.

"It's just a thing you discover," said
Christopher Robin carelessly, not
being quite sure himself.

"Oh! I see. Are bears any good at
discovering it?"

"Of course they are," said Christopher Robin. "And Rabbit and Kanga and all of you. That's what an expedition means. A long line of everybody. You'd better tell the others to get ready. And we must all bring provisions."

A little while later, they
were all ready at the edge
of the forest and the
Expotition started.

First came Christopher Robin
and Rabbit, then Piglet and Pooh,
then Kanga, with Roo in her pocket,
and Owl, then Eeyore, and at the
end, in a long line, all Rabbit's
friends and relations.

"I didn't ask them," explained Rabbit
carelessly. "They just came. They
always do. They can march at the end,
after Eeyore."

There was a shout from the top of the line.

"Come on!" called Christopher Robin.

"We're starting," said Rabbit. "I must go." And he hurried off to the front of the Expotition.

So off they all went to discover the
North Pole. And as they walked, they
chattered to each other of this and
that, all except Pooh, who was making
up a song.

Pooh began to sing:

"They all went off to discover the Pole,
　Owl and Piglet and Rabbit and all;
It's a thing you discover, as I've been tole
　By Owl and Piglet and Rabbit and all.
Eeyore, Christopher Robin and Pooh
And Rabbit's relations all went too –
And where the Pole was none of them knew...
　Sing Hey! for Owl and Rabbit and all!"

"Hush!" said Christopher Robin, turning round to Pooh. "We're just coming to a dangerous place."

"Hush!" "*Hush!*" they all said hastily to each other all down the line, until it got to the last one of all.

Hush!

Hush!

Hush!

And the last and smallest friend-and-relation was so upset to find that the whole Expotition was saying "Hush!" to him, that he buried himself in a crack in the ground and stayed there for two whole days until the danger was over!

They had come to a stream which
twisted and tumbled between high
rocky banks, and Christopher Robin
saw at once how dangerous it was.

"It's just the place," he explained, "for an ambush."

"What sort of bush?" whispered Pooh to Piglet. "A gorse bush?"

"My dear Pooh," said Owl, "an ambush is a sort of surprise. We are not *talking* about gorse bushes..."

"I am," said Pooh.

After a while, they came to a place where the banks of the stream widened out on each side, and there was a level strip of grass on which they could rest.

As soon as he saw this, Christopher Robin called, "Halt!" and they all sat down and rested.

"I think that we ought to eat all our provisions now, so that we shan't have so much to carry."

"That's a good idea," said Pooh, and Eeyore looked around for some thistles to eat.

As soon as he had finished lunch,
Christopher Robin whispered to
Rabbit, and they walked a little way
up the stream.

"I didn't want the others to hear," he
said. "Rabbit, I don't suppose *you*
know what the North Pole *looks* like,
do you?"

"Well," said Rabbit, "I suppose it's just a pole stuck in the ground."

"Yes, that's what I thought."

"*Where is it sticking?*" puzzled Rabbit.

"That's what we're looking for," said Christopher Robin, still rather baffled, as they walked back to the others.

Everyone had finished eating and Baby Roo was washing his face and paws in the stream.

Suddenly, there came a squeak from Roo, a splash and a loud cry of alarm from Kanga.

"Roo's fallen in!" cried Rabbit, and they all rushed to the rescue.

"Look at me swimming!" squeaked Roo, and down he went over the next waterfall into another pool.

"Get something across the stream lower down," called Rabbit.

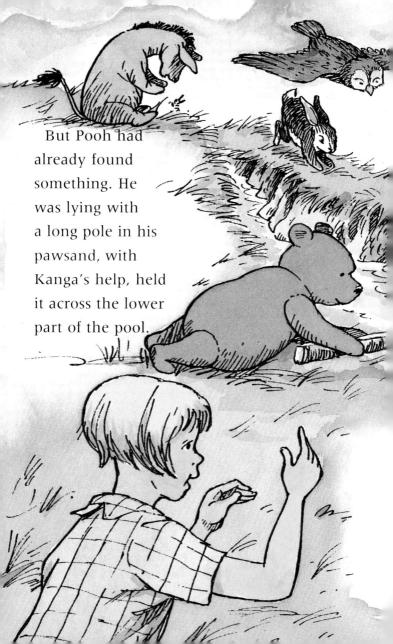

But Pooh had
already found
something. He
was lying with
a long pole in his
pawsand, with
Kanga's help, held
it across the lower
part of the pool.

And Roo drifted up against it and
climbed out.

"Did you see me swimming?" squeaked
Roo.

But Christopher Robin
wasn't listening. "Pooh,"
he said, "where did you find
that pole?"

"I just found it," he said, looking at it.

"Pooh," said Christopher Robin. "You
have found the North Pole!"

"Is that what we were looking for?" asked Eeyore.

"Yes," said a proud Pooh.

They stuck the pole in the ground and Christopher Robin tied a message on to it. Then they all went home again.

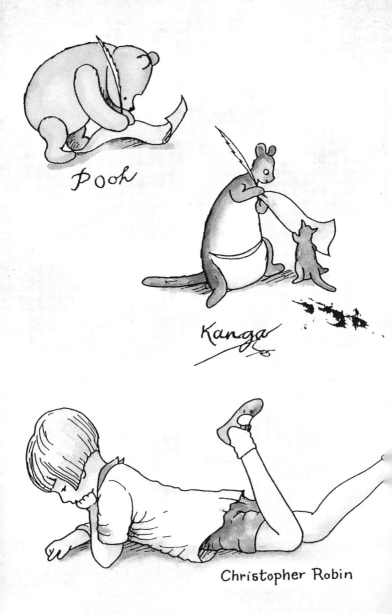

Pooh

Kanga

Christopher Robin